Amalia AND THE Grasshopper

Written by Jerry Tello

Illustrated by Loretta Krupinski

SCHOLASTIC INC.

New York   Toronto   London   Auckland   Sydney

Copyright © 1994 by Scholastic Inc.
All rights reserved. Published by Scholastic Inc.
Printed in the U.S.A.
ISBN 0-590-27533-X

20 19   09   00

It was early in the morning and
Amalia was already outside playing
basketball. She was six years old and
she liked basketball very much.

She wanted to be like her big brother Marcos, who was a very good basketball player.

Yet as hard as Amalia tried, the
ball never went high enough to make
a basket. Every day she would shoot,
and every day she would miss.

She would shoot from the left,

from the right,

and from the middle.

The more she would shoot,
the more she would miss.

For luck one day, Amalia even put
on her big brother's basketball shirt.

Yet the more she would shoot,
the more she would miss.

Then one day, when Amalia's grandfather came to visit, he saw Amalia was sad.

"What's wrong, Amalia?" asked
her grandfather.

"Every day I come outside
and shoot, and all I do is miss.
I'm just too little," said Amalia.

Amalia's grandfather hugged
her and said, "Look over there
by that tree."

"It's a little grasshopper," said
Amalia.

"Look and see what it does,"
said her grandfather.

Just then, the grasshopper
jumped very far.

"Wow!" said Amalia. "It jumped far."

"And how did it jump so far?"
asked her grandfather.

"With its legs," said Amalia.

"Now come here," said her
grandfather. He showed Amalia
how to bend and push off with
her legs.

"Try it," said her grandfather.

So Amalia bent her legs, and
as she pushed off with her legs,
she threw the ball at the basket.

The ball went way up and hit
the rim—but it didn't go in.

"Try again," said her grandfather.
"But this time pretend you have
grasshopper legs and push off
really hard."

This time Amalia bent her legs
and pushed off really hard as she
let the ball go.

The ball went way up and then
swish into the basket.

Amalia was so happy, she jumped
up and down and had a big smile on
her face. She was so happy that she
didn't hear her brother Marcos clapping.

As Marcos came over to give Amalia
a high-five, their grandfather said, "Hey,
look at the basketball."

There, sitting on top of the
basketball was the grasshopper.
Amalia crept over as quietly as she
could. "Thanks," she whispered.
But the grasshopper pushed off with
its legs and jumped out of sight.